AVALANCHE ALERT

J. BURCHETT & S. VOGLER

STONE ARCH BOOKS
a capstone imprint

Wild Rescue books are published by Stone Arch Books
A Capstone Imprint
1710 Roe Crest Drive
North Mankato, Minnesota 56003
www.capstonepub.com

First published by Stripes Publishing Ltd.
1 The Coda Centre
189 Munster Road
London SW6 6AW
© Jan Burchett and Sara Vogler, 2012
Interior art © Diane Le Feyer of Cartoon Saloon, 2012

Cataloging-in-Publication Data is available at the Library of Congress website.

ISBN: 978-1-4342-3772-9 (library binding)

Summary: Following an avalanche in the Himalayas, a snow leopard and her
cub have been separated from their territory and forced to eat sheep from a
nearby village in order to survive. But now the locals have plans to protect their
livestock by poisoning the leopards! The twins must brave sub-zero temperatures
and treacherous slopes to find the elusive cats and guide them to safety.

Cover Art: Sam Kennedy
Graphic Designer: Russell Griesmer
Production Specialist: Michelle Biedscheid

Design Credits: Shutterstock 51686107 (p. 4-5),
Shutterstock 51614464 (back cover, p. 148-149, 150, 152)

Printed in the United States of America in Stevens Point, Wisconsin.
012013   007118R

TABLE OF CONTENTS

WILD RESCUE

MISSION

BEN WOODWARD
WILD Operative

ZOE WOODWARD
WILD Operative

PRINCE

TARGET: ◎

BRIEFING

CHAPTER 1

WILD WEATHER

"Here comes the sandstorm!" Ben yelled. "Take cover!"

Zoe pulled on her goggles and gave her twin brother a thumbs-up. Immediately, they were blasted with stinging sand and hot wind. They turned their backs to the wind and huddled together, pulling their shirts over their faces.

"Had enough?" yelled Ben.

Zoe nodded. "Yeah," she said. "Let's put an end to this."

Her brother pressed a button on the remote control in his hand. The sandstorm stopped as suddenly as it had begun. Zoe brushed herself off. Small vents opened in the wall next to them, quickly sucking the sand away.

"Uncle Stephen is amazing!" Zoe said. She took the remote and examined all its functions. "This new climate chamber might be his most impressive invention yet."

"And it's really going to help us prepare for our missions," agreed Ben. "We've had missions in a desert, a rainforest, and high atop a mountain."

"The thin air up there wasn't much fun," Zoe said, referring to their mountaintop adventure. "It made me feel light-headed and dizzy."

"What's new?" teased her brother. He darted out of the way as Zoe tried to give him a friendly punch. "So what else can we do with the climate chamber?"

Ben and Zoe were spending their winter vacation at the top secret underground headquarters of WILD. Their uncle, Dr. Stephen Fisher, ran the place. It was dedicated to rescuing animals in danger all over the world, and the twins were its youngest recruits. No one except their grandma was in on the secret. Even their parents didn't know that when Uncle Stephen called, Ben and Zoe dropped everything for one of WILD's important missions.

"How about this?" Zoe grinned and pointed to a green button marked MONSOON.

A shrill buzzer sounded from a loudspeaker, followed by a familiar voice. "Urgent! Ben and Zoe, report to the Control Room immediately!"

"Uncle Stephen sounds anxious," Zoe said. "What do you think he wants?"

Ben chuckled. "He probably just can't wait to hear what we think of his climate chamber."

Ben and Zoe raced down the long hallway, past the labs, the cafeteria, and sleeping quarters. They slapped their hands on the ID pad outside the Control Room.

"Print ID confirmed," came the electronic voice. The metal door slid open smoothly, revealing the brightly lit room that was the headquarters of WILD. Workers were tapping away at computers.

Images of animals were everywhere on the giant monitors lining both sides of the room. At the far end, Uncle Stephen was staring at a display screen on the wall. He wore a labcoat over his shorts, and his hat was pushed back in his messy hair.

"Your climate chamber's great!" said Zoe.

"Yeah!" agreed Ben. "The sandstorm is —" He went silent. Uncle Stephen was staring intently at the screen in front of him, a worried look on his face.

"What's the matter?" Zoe asked her uncle.

"Erika just picked up some alarming intelligence," said Uncle Stephen gravely. "No more fun in the climate chamber — you're off on a mission. There's no time to waste."

"Good thing we're here, then," said Ben.

"Are you going to give us a clue to the animal we'll be rescuing?" asked Zoe. Uncle Stephen usually presented a glass eyeball to the twins so they would have to guess what their mission was.

Uncle Stephen turned to his assistant, Erika Bohn, a woman sitting nearby. She swung around in her chair to face them. "No time for an eyeball," she said, tapping a key, "but this might clue you in."

A picture of an animal eye flashed up on the screen in front of her.

"There's fur around it," muttered Zoe. "Is it a wolf?"

"Not a bad guess," Erika said. She scrolled out so that a little more of the animal was visible.

"Its fur is light brown with black markings," said Ben. "And it looks thick."

"So the animal lives somewhere cold," said Zoe.

Uncle Stephen nodded. "Extremely cold," he said.

"It looks like the eye of a big cat," said Ben.

Uncle Stephen nodded. "A very rare one," he added.

"A snow leopard!" cried Zoe.

Their uncle nodded and smiled. "Correct!" he said.

Ben gave a whistle. "They are extremely endangered," he said. "And hardly ever seen by people." He turned to Zoe. "Did you know their tails are as long as their bodies?"

Zoe laughed. "Thank you, Mr. Encyclopedia!" she said. "But you forgot to mention they can carry up to three times their own weight." She turned to their uncle. "So what happened to this snow leopard?"

"We have a computer program set to flag up certain key words on the Internet," Uncle Stephen explained. "It flagged a blog from a mountaineer in Himachal Pradesh."

"I know where that is," Zoe said before Ben could open his mouth. "The Indian Himalayas."

"Precisely, Zoe," Uncle Stephen said. He brought up a satellite map of India on the screen and pointed toward a line of jagged white peaks running across the top corner.

"I've been checking on the blog for a week now," Erika said, pointing.

Erika clicked on a post halfway down the page. "The mountaineer has been staying in a village called Ribek and climbing in the peaks a few miles west from there," she said. "While he was climbing, he caught a glimpse of a snow leopard sleeping in a rock shelter."

"Lucky him!" said Ben. "Hardly anyone gets to see one."

"Not just one," Erika said. "Four! A mother and three cubs." She clicked a button on the keyboard. "Here's a photo he put up on his blog."

An image of a large leopard and three fuzzy cubs popped up on the screen. The mother leopard slept with her tail wrapped around her three sleeping cubs. Her fur was covered in a beautiful pattern of dark circular spots with lighter fur in the middle.

"Aw!" Zoe said. "They're so cute."

"I estimate the cubs to be four or five months old," their uncle said. "The mountaineer called the mother Rani, which means 'queen' in Hindi."

"Three cubs is good," said Zoe. "She's helping to repopulate the species in that region."

"If they all survive," Uncle Stephen interjected. He brought up the mountaineer's blog on the screen. "His last blog post was was early this morning."

As the words appeared on the screen, Ben and Zoe gasped in horror. "Yesterday there was a massive avalanche!" read Ben.

CHAPTER 2

FANG

"Are all the leopards okay?" Zoe asked.

"It says here that the avalanche came down on the eastern edge of the protected area," their uncle said. "They could have been caught in it."

Ben read quickly. "He posted that he saw Rani again last night, with one cub, but this time far from her territory," Ben said. "She was close to Ribek, and that's around twenty miles away from her home. Poor Rani! What happened to the others?"

"Maybe this is a different leopard," suggested Zoe.

"Very unlikely, Zoe," said Erika. "There are so few leopards left that it has to be Rani."

"She probably panicked when the avalanche struck and just ran away," said Uncle Stephen. "It's likely that her route back to her territory was blocked."

"And only one cub went with her," said Ben.

"Indeed," their uncle said. "With any luck, the other two cubs are safe on the far side of the avalanche. But we can't be sure."

"Will they be all right without their mother?" asked Zoe, eyes wide.

"Not for long," said Erika.

"They barely know how to fend for themselves," Uncle Stephen added, "so they still need their mother to survive."

"Won't Rani find her own way back?" asked Ben.

"She might eventually," said Uncle Stephen, "but we're running out of time. It's not only the two cubs that are the problem. Rani has now been seen near the village. Snow leopards don't usually go near human habitation unless they can't find food in the wild. She's probably stealing the village livestock for food."

"The villagers are very poor," Erika added. "They can't afford to lose their animals."

"So they might kill Rani and her cub for taking their sole source of food for the winter," said Uncle Stephen.

"Then our mission is to get Rani and her baby home to the rest of her family," said Zoe, "and as soon as possible!"

"That's the idea," said Erika. She switched the display back to the satellite map and pointed to Ribek. "Your route will take you west from the village, across the mountains, and into the protected territory."

Ben frowned. "The most direct route would be across the avalanche field," he said, "but I'm guessing it's too risky."

Their uncle nodded.

"We'll go above it, then," said Zoe. "It looks like there's a ridge there. You ready for some serious mountain climbing, bro?"

"You know it, sis," Ben said. "After all, we're experts on the WILD climbing wall!"

"This is going to be much harder than the climbing wall," said Erika. "The terrain is very hostile in the Himalayas. It's extremely cold, and the loose snow can make the going even more treacherous."

"We'll be able to handle it," Ben said confidently. "One thing bothers me, though — how do we get the snow leopards to follow us? They're wild animals. We can't just put them on a leash."

"Don't worry about that," said Uncle Stephen. "You're going to lure them back. I modified your BUGs to fire capsules that burst on impact and release a strong scent of sheep, their favorite food."

Uncle Stephen handed Ben and Zoe their BUGs — Brilliant Undercover Gizmos. They were equipped with satellite maps, tracking devices, translators, and many more amazing tools. Ben and Zoe never went on a mission without them.

"Just pull up that nozzle on the side, press this button, and one of the scent bombs will shoot out," Uncle Stephen explained. "You can set the distance you want them to travel. They have a range of a few hundred yards, so you can keep your distance. After all, you don't want to be Rani's next meal!"

"And that's not the only new device your uncle has invented," Erika said. She pointed at two small cylinders lying on the table next to her keyboard. Next to them was a pair of harnesses.

"The FANG!" said Uncle Stephen. "Also known as the Fisher Avalanche Nano Gun. It'll be very useful if you happen to get buried in an avalanche." Ben and Zoe exchanged worried glances. "The gadget attaches to the back of your climbing helmet," Uncle Stephen continued. "You pull the emergency cord here on your harness and a line shoots up, making an air hole. When it reaches the surface, a small umbrella opens over the snow."

"The umbrella stops the line from slipping back down the hole and from filling up with snow," said Erika.

"Then a beacon flashes on top of the umbrella to alert a rescuer!" their uncle finished.

"Cool!" Ben said.

Uncle Stephen grinned. "Cool, indeed!" he said. "You could say that your new FANGs are . . . FANG-tastic."

Ben groaned at his uncle's terrible pun.

"It's unlikely there'll be another avalanche, right?" asked Zoe.

"It could happen," said Dr. Fisher. "The mountaineer said the snow was hard-packed ice. A heavy snowfall on that kind of surface would be more likely to slide down as an avalanche."

"An avalanche movie is on the WILD Jet's computer," Erika said. "There'll be time to watch it during the flight to India."

Zoe was reading the blog again. "What about Rani's other cubs?" she asked. "They need help as well."

"That's where I come in," said Erika. "The minute you're packed, we'll be off to India in the WILD jet. Once I've dropped you off, I'm going to fly over the leopards' home and search for the youngsters using heat-seeking equipment. I'm planning to drop them some food to help them survive until their mother returns."

Uncle Stephen led the way to the stockroom. Erika passed Ben and Zoe their backpacks, veterinary kits, snowsuits, thermal gloves, climbing helmets, ice axes, and special boots.

"The boots have retractable spikes for ice climbing," said Uncle Stephen.

"Nice!" said Zoe.

"Are we parachuting in?" Ben asked
hopefully.

"Not quite!" their uncle said, chuckling.
"You're taking the local bus! If anyone asks
why you're on your own, you'll say you're
joining your aunt, Erika, who's staying at
the nearby monastery."

"A bus doesn't sound very quick," said
Ben.

"The village and the snow leopard's terrain are high in the mountains," explained Erika. "In fact, the road is the only access route. You'll need to get used to the altitude, and the bus journey is perfect for that. You'd better sleep on the plane, because you'll be up at night once your mission starts. Don't forget, that's when Rani will be most active since Indian snow leopards are nocturnal."

"Are you ready?" their uncle asked them.

"You bet!" Ben and Zoe said together.

CHAPTER 3
ASCENT

Zoe gripped the handrail tightly as the bus hit another pothole. She bumped into Ben. "Sorry!" she said. "That's another bruise for the collection."

They were crammed between five other people on the bus's back seat with their backpacks on their laps. Erika had dropped them off at a private airfield in a remote spot in the Himalayan mountains' foothills.

Now, the ramshackle old bus was taking them up to Ribek, the village where the climber had reported seeing Rani and her cub.

Zoe shifted her position on the hard wooden seat. "This is a pretty big change after the comfy plane ride," she whispered to Ben.

The bus sputtered and roared as it made its way up the steep road with its many twists and turns. A fierce river rushed past, crashing over rocks and boulders. Then the road took another turn. All around Ben and Zoe, the local people chatted and laughed loudly.

"Better put in our translators," whispered Ben. He reached into his backpack and peeled the small plastic earpiece off his BUG. Then he popped it in his ear.

Zoe did the same. She scrolled as quickly as the jolting bus would allow through the menu on her BUG, searching for the Pahari language. Erika had told her that there were many dialects of it spoken here in Himachal Pradesh, but that the BUG could handle it. Zoe hoped so.

She peered out of the window. The bus was crawling around a hairpin bend. She got a dizzying glimpse of the sheer drop below. This was the sort of terrain that she and Ben were going to be climbing. For the first time, Zoe realized how difficult this mission was going to be.

Ben was sitting next to two women. One of them reached into a basket and pulled out something wrapped in a cloth. She unpeeled the package, producing some smelly cheese and lumps of brown bread.

The woman handed them to her companion and then nudged Ben. Her lined face broke into a huge grin as she offered him some of their meal.

Ben took some, nodded his thanks and ate hungrily. The cheese was strong, but the bread was delicious.

"It's fried," Ben told Zoe, handing her a piece.

The woman smiled and turned back to her companion and continuted to chat. They both seemed concerned that her yogurt might be going bad.

Just then, Zoe realized she was breathing more quickly than usual. "We must be getting very high up in the mountains now," she said. "I can feel it."

"Well, don't go stumbling around like you did in the climate chamber," Ben said with a laugh.

The bus rounded another bend in the road. For a second, it leaned as if it had tipped onto two wheels. Everyone was flung from one side to the other.

Ben groaned. "Now who's feeling funny?" asked Zoe.

The woman next to Ben dug into her pocket and produced a piece of candy wrapped in paper. She held it out and Ben took it gratefully. He sat there, chewing and holding his head in his hands.

The men on Zoe's right were having a conversation about the weather. The older of the two, a gray-haired man with a bushy beard, was shaking his head and looking worried. "I think it will snow again before long," he said.

His companion nervously pulled at the fringes of his heavy coat. "That might cause another avalanche," he said in a worried tone. "And look what the first one brought us!"

The older man scratched his beard and nodded. "Too true," he said.

"The winter will be hard enough without that snow leopard eating all our animals," said the younger one. "It took one of my goats last night. I heard the cries from the house, but by the time I got out there, it was too out of sight."

Zoe tensed and listened. *They must be talking about Rani,* she thought.

"There's only one thing to be done," the man continued. "And it has to be done tonight before it helps itself to more of my herd. I'll leave it some fresh meat laced with poison. That will stop that leopard for good."

CHAPTER 4

POISON

"Did you hear that?" Zoe whispered to Ben. "They're going to poison Rani tonight. We can't let that happen!"

Ben nodded. "We've got to get to the snow leopards first and lure them away before they get a scent of that meat," he said.

The man was still speaking to his elderly companion. "I don't want to poison a wild animal, but I haven't got the money to build an indoor shelter for my goats."

Pretending to concentrate on the passing view, Zoe listened intently. It seemed clear that the men had no idea that Rani had a cub with her.

"Shame your house is right on the edge of the village," said the older man. "It leaves your goats vulnerable and unprotected."

"Not tonight," replied the goat owner. "I'll make sure that wild animal is dead before it gets its paws on my goats."

Zoe's eyes went wide with fear. "The first thing we need to do," she whispered to Ben, "is find out exactly where those goats are."

* * *

After a long trip, the bus rattled to a stop on the outer edge of a small village.

On either side of the rough road were straight lined, white walled houses with thatch-covered roofs. Ben and Zoe slung on their backpacks and filed to the door of the bus, following the busy locals. In the distance, they saw the towering peaks of the snow-covered mountains looming large.

As they jumped down from the bus, freezing air stung their faces. Zoe pulled up her hood. She was glad that their super-warm snowsuits and thermal gloves did a lot to block the freezing cold wind.

"Just walk along confidently like you know where you're going," Ben whispered to Zoe. "That way, we won't attract attention."

Zoe nodded. "Remember our cover story," she said. "We're going to meet our aunt, who's staying at the local monastery."

The bus pulled away, its engine roaring. Ben turned back to look at the other passengers who'd left the bus. They were scurrying toward their homes. The owner of the goats said goodbye to his companion, and then hurried down the road. Ben started to follow him.

Zoe grabbed Ben's arm. "Are you crazy?" she whispered. "We can't just creep after him like a couple of spies! He would probably notice."

"I wasn't going to creep," Ben said. "I was going to walk along confidently — just like I said. We've got to find out where he lives."

Zoe saw a woman looking at them with concern.

"Are you lost?" the woman asked in Pahari. The BUG translated her words.

Zoe smiled and shrugged, pretending she didn't understand the woman. Thinking quickly, she peered into the distance and then gave a big wave as if she'd seen someone. She dragged Ben away. He hadn't seen her little bit of play-acting, and protested. "What are you doing?" he asked.

"Look, it's Auntie!" said Zoe, tugging Ben's arm.

Then Ben realized what Zoe was doing. He waved an arm enthusiastically as Zoe marched him down a narrow path next to a gleaming white Hindu temple.

"Let's get to the end of this path," Zoe said. "Then we'll work out what to do."

"Better be quick," warned Ben. "It's nearly dusk, so Rani will soon be on the prowl."

They crept around the back of the elaborate stone temple and found themselves among a group of trees that were hung with bright cloths. The ragged banners flapped overhead in the cold wind.

"Here's the plan," said Zoe. "We know the goat pen is on the edge of the village, so we'll head there. Then we find the meat and get rid of it."

"And then we get on with our original mission to lure Rani away and back to her territory," Ben said. "Better update Uncle Stephen."

Zoe pressed her BUG hot key to call WILD headquarters.

"What news do you have?" said Uncle Stephen.

Zoe told him what they'd learned on the bus. "Poison? Oh, dear," said Uncle Stephen. "Monkshood is what hunters used to put on their spear tips. It's lethal, even if it touches skin — leopard or human."

"Do you know if there's an antidote?" asked Zoe. "Just in case?"

"I'll let you know as soon as I've found it," said their uncle.

"Have you heard from Erika?" Ben asked. "Did she find the other cubs?"

"There's no word from Erika yet," said Uncle Stephen.

Zoe looked up at the darkening sky. "Better say goodbye for now," she said. "We have to get going. Talk to you soon, Uncle Stephen. Over and out."

* * *

Keeping to the lengthening shadows, Ben and Zoe emerged from the trees and skirted around the edge of the village. They followed the dark tracks between the small houses. As the light faded, the tall, jagged mountain peaks stood out against the glow of sunset.

Ben stopped and listened. "I hear goats!" he said. "And it sounds like they're right ahead of us."

They crept past the last of the houses toward a small wooden shed. The bleating was coming from a fenced enclosure not far ahead. Beyond was a line of fir trees that marked the edge of a small forest stretching up the steep mountainside. They could barely see the snowline high above it.

As they moved near the shed, they could hear animals chewing their cud.

"These must be the ones," said Zoe. "The farmer said he was right at the edge of the village near the forest by the mountains."

Ben looked off into the distance with an alarmed look on his face. "Someone's coming!" he whispered.

Zoe glanced where Ben was looking. "It's the man from the bus," she said. "Quick, we need to hide!"

CHAPTER 5

SPOTTED

Ben and Zoe peered around the corner of the shed. A moment later, the goat owner stepped out from the darkness of the trees. He held a flashlight in one hand and an empty plastic bag in the other. He opened the shed door, and emerged a few moments later carrying a metal bucket. He tipped the contents over the fence into a stone trough in the goats' pen. He watched the animals gather around the food and eat, and then he walked slowly toward the nearest house.

The man shined his flashlight into the dark shadows as he walked. Ben and Zoe shrank back to avoid being seen.

At last they heard the bang of a wooden door shutting. Slowly, the twins crept toward the enclosure.

"I'm setting my BUG to detect snow leopard calls," whispered Zoe. "That way we'll pick up any sounds Rani makes and be warned if she comes close."

"Meanwhile, we find the meat and get rid of it," said Ben. "You go one way around the goats' pen and I'll take the other. It can't be far away."

Bent double to keep out of sight, the twins moved along opposite sides of the fence, searching the ground. The goats bleated at them, hoping for more food.

Shielding her flashlight so only a tiny amount of light came out, Zoe searched the ground. Soon she saw Ben again.

"There's no sign of the meat," Ben whispered.

"Maybe the man didn't use any poison after all," said Zoe.

Just then, there was a faint, high-pitched mewling sound from somewhere among the trees. Zoe's BUG vibrated in her hand and "snow leopard" appeared on the screen.

"That must be Rani!" said Ben. "She's on her way."

Zoe gasped. "When we saw the man, he was coming from the forest," she said. "Maybe he put the poison there — not here!"

"You're right," Ben said. "He was holding an empty bag. He must have been using it to carry the poisoned meat. Quick, we've got to find it before Rani does!"

As quietly as they could, the twins headed for the trees.

"Night vision goggles on," Ben reminded Zoe.

They slipped their slim goggles over their eyes. The dark trunks now stood out clearly in a green glow.

"And scent dispersers," added Zoe, activating her BUG to mask her smell. She didn't want to scare Rani away — or become her next dinner! Ben did the same.

"Over here!" whispered Zoe. "Something's moving."

They crept forward silently.

Ahead of them, the slim shape of a big cat padded down toward them through the trees.

"Here she comes!" Zoe whispered excitedly.

The snow leopard stopped, raised her head, and sniffed the air. Through the goggles, Zoe could see the large, dark prints on the leopard's body and smaller, lighter ones on her head. She padded elegantly along on her wide paws, her long tail swishing behind her.

"She's beautiful!" said Zoe. "How could anyone even consider poisoning her?"

Rani raised her head suspiciously at the slight sound. "She may not be able to smell us, but she can hear us!" Ben whispered in Zoe's ear. "Don't move, and speak quietly."

"Looks like she hasn't found the bait yet," Zoe whispered back. "But where's her cub?"

"There's movement a little farther up the slope," said Ben. He zoomed in with his goggles. Now he could make out a much smaller shape trotting along behind. "Her cub is following her. Forget finding the poison. We need to get them away from here."

Zoe's fingers tapped her BUG's keys. "I'll get ready to fire a scent bomb," she said.

Ben was focusing intently on the young snow leopard. "The cub's running ahead of its mom now," he whispered. "It's sniffing at something. Oh — what if it's the poison?!"

Without thinking, Ben ran into the clearing, yelling and waving his hands.

The two big cats were immediately alert, heads raised and ears raised. The next second, they vanished back into the forest, the cub scampering after its mother.

"You did it!" said Zoe, running after her brother. "Now we have to lure them away."

But the movement in the forest had spooked the goats in the pen. They burst into a chorus of nervous bleating.

"That might be a problem," Ben said.

Then the twins heard a door open, followed by angry voices.

Ben and Zoe froze. Their hearts beat wildly.

"The goat owner is back!" whispered Ben. "And there's someone else with him."

Zoe and Ben hid behind a jagged rock and laid flat on their bellies. A flashlight beam zigzagged around the trees. They covered their eyes. If their goggles reflected the light, it would give them away.

Footsteps were coming close to their position. As soon as the beam of light had swept past, Ben risked a glance.

Two men were pushing through the trees toward them. They had big sticks in their hands, using them to slash at bushes and ferns as they walked past.

"Stay down!" whispered Zoe.

CHAPTER 6

ON TRACK

The men looked around. Ben and Zoe could hear their footsteps crunching on the scattered pinecones of the forest floor. Now they were leaning against the rock, just inches away from Ben and Zoe.

"Some of the meat's been eaten," said a voice, the translated words coming through loud and clear in their earpieces.

Ben felt Zoe stiffen next to him.

"Hopefully that's the last we'll see of that beast," said the other man.

"It doesn't take much for the poison to work," the other man said. "We'd better bury the meat deep so that nothing else eats the monkshood."

Ben and Zoe heard the footsteps go up the slope. Ben craned his neck to see a man pick up the meat with the end of his stick.

"Don't let it touch your skin," said the other man. "Even that could poison you. And burn that wood after you're done."

"I will," the man holding the stick said. "Don't worry."

After what seemed like forever, the men went back into the house.

Ben and Zoe scrambled out from their hiding place. "We've got to find Rani," said Ben. "The men said some of the meat had been eaten. I bet the cub ate it."

They raced up the slope to where the meat had been. Zoe shined her flashlight over the ground. There were paw prints in the soft earth under the trees. She called up the paw prints of a snow leopard on her BUG.

"Looks like a perfect match," she said. "Four small pads with a larger one behind. At least we can track them now."

"Has she left her scent anywhere?" asked Ben. "I read about that on the plane. Snow leopards rub against rocks to leave a marking trail."

"Good thinking. I'll check," said Zoe. She tapped the BUG's display and switched programs. "Yep — it's picking up a strong snow leopard scent!"

"Let's get going then," Ben said.

Following the prints and scent, they walked up the hill to the last of the trees. Now the terrain was open, steep, and rocky. There were patches of earth here and there with small plants growing from them. Every now and then, a solitary fir tree rose up from of the darkness.

Ben studied the rocky ground. "I don't see any more prints," he said. "There aren't any scratch marks here, either."

"No scent either," Zoe said. "Are we going in the wrong direction?" She held her BUG toward the ground and swept it around in a circle, trying to pick up Rani's scent. For a second, it vibrated, but then went still. "It's very faint, but at least it's a signal. Looks like she's gone northeast." Zoe pointed to a steep wall of rock ahead that was cut by natural ledges.

Ben and Zoe made their way to the base of the rock. "We've got a hard climb ahead of us," said Ben.

Using cracks in the rocks as handholds and footholds, they scrambled up the stone face until they reached a wide shelf. They stood there for a moment, catching their breaths.

They scanned the area, looking for any sign of the snow leopards.

A full moon came out from behind the clouds, casting a faint glow on the deep crevices of the Himalayas. They walked along the shelf until it flattened out into a shallow valley. Its sides were marked by jagged rocks and low bushes.

"They could be anywhere," said Zoe.

Then they both saw it. A creature was padding across the valley floor.

"It's Rani!" whispered Ben.

"But where's her cub?" Zoe whispered back.

"She's carrying it in her mouth," Ben told her. "And it looks like it's unconscious." Zoe could see the alarm on his face. He added, "I hope we're not too late."

CHAPTER 7

ANTIDOTE

Rani laid her lifeless cub down in the shelter of an overhang of rock. She prowled anxiously around it, on guard for any threats.

"I wish Uncle Stephen would get back to us with the antidote," said Zoe. "It might just be in time to save the poor little thing — if we can even get to it."

Keeping low, they crept forward and took cover behind a thick, prickly bush.

Ben's BUG vibrated. "Message from WILD," he told his sister. He read it quickly. "The antidote is atropine. It says here the poison will have slowed the cub's heart rate and this is our only hope of restoring it. But where do we find atropine? It's not like there's a pharmacy up here."

Zoe took his BUG and looked at the message. "You didn't scroll down, did you?" she said, annoyed. "Look — it says, 'You'll find some atropine in your vet kit.'"

Ben frowned. "Then let's get on with it," he said.

Zoe looked over at Rani. The snow leopard was nuzzling her baby. "And face a fully grown snow leopard protecting her cub?" she said. "No way. And I don't think she'll leave her cub for any reason right now other than to hunt prey."

Ben smiled. "Then we have to make her think there's prey," he said. He punched some keys on the BUG.

"You've got that look again," Zoe said with a worried frown. "You're going to do something risky, aren't you?"

Ben pulled out the scent bomb nozzle and aimed the BUG toward a boulder a ways away from them. "I'll fire this and lure her away," he said. "As soon as the coast's clear, you go and give the cub the atropine."

"Be careful!" said Zoe. "Whatever you do, keep out of sight or you could be helping Rani to a real supper — especially if she thinks her cub is in danger."

Rani's head shot up as she caught a whiff of the scent of sheep.

We don't want her rushing over there, so I'm going to give her something to stalk," Ben said. He pressed a button on his BUG. An image of a holographic sheep began to form in the dark.

Zoe gazed around them doubtfully. "You'll be in a lot of danger, Ben," she said. "You won't be able to get very far from Rani in this terrain."

"I don't have a choice," said Ben firmly. "And don't worry, I have my scent disperser on."

Zoe shrugged. She knew that it was pointless to try to stop Ben from doing something when he had his mind made up. "If you manage to avoid getting eaten, try and fire a tracking dart into her," she said dryly. "I'll do the same to the cub."

"Good idea," Ben said with a grin.

Ben sped off, keeping out of sight and moving the holographic image along the rock. Rani began to stalk on her belly after her prey.

With the vet kit in her hand, Zoe crept up to the cub and gasped. It was such a beautiful little creature, with its thick spotted coat and its dark eyes. Zoe shook herself back into focus. She had a job to do, and it was urgent. The cub seemed to be barely breathing.

Zoe fumbled for the syringe and sucked up atropine from the little vial in the case. She gently took a handful of loose skin on the cub's neck, lifting the little creature up. It barely stirred as she eased the needle into its flesh.

Zoe wished that there was more she could do. The cub was just lying there, so weak and helpless. But now, all she could do was wait — and hope. She stroked the soft fur, admiring its beautiful pattern of spots.

"Come on," she whispered. "Get better, little prince." She smiled to herself. "That's what I'll call you — Prince!"

Quickly scrolling through the BUG menu, Zoe started the tracking program. She moved back a bit, then fired a dart into Prince's thick belly fur. At once, an orange light began flashing on the screen.

"We won't lose you now," she said, reluctantly sneaking back to a safe distance. She wished she could stay with him, but she knew that Rani would be back at any moment.

Ben scrambled along a ridge at the edge of the valley, projecting the hologram as far away from himself as he could. The snow leopard moved stealthily after it, nose raised, picking up the sheep scent from the BUG.

So far, his plan was working well. Rani was so close now that he could see all her beautiful markings quite clearly, as well as her rippling muscles. He crouched, playing the hologram slowly along the rocks. Now was the time to fire a tracking dart. But as the dart hit home, Rani suddenly turned and headed straight for him!

There was no time to react. Ben cowered, arms covering his head, as Rani pounced into the air.

CHAPTER 8

HIGH GROUND

THUD! Ben heard the snow leopard land very close. Any second now, he'd feel her claws carving into his back. But just then he heard a sharp squeal of pain nearby. Ben peeked between his fingers. Rani was slinking off over the rocks with a hare in her jaws. She was taking the food back to her cub. Ben picked up his BUG, turned off the hologram, and followed. After that scare, he made sure to keep his distance.

There was no time to warn Zoe. He hoped she'd had long enough to give the cub the antidote — and get away safely.

Soon he could see the snow leopard cub lying under the ledge. To his relief, Zoe wasn't there. Its mother bounded to its side and, dropping the hare, nudged her baby gently with her nose. She pushed her offering toward her cub, but it didn't react at all.

Zoe was crouching behind a rock a few yards away. "Am I relieved to see you!" she whispered as her brother ducked down beside her. "For a moment, I wasn't sure what Rani had in her jaws."

Ben let out a snort of laughter. "You thought it might be a little chunk of me, didn't you?"

"Well, if Rani is really hungry, then she won't be picky," Zoe said.

"How's the cub?" asked Ben. "Did you manage to give it the antidote?"

Zoe nodded. "And the cub's a little male, not an it," she said. "I've decided to name him Prince."

"Let's hope the medicine's not too late for little Prince," Ben said. "It doesn't look like he's moved."

"You're too impatient," Zoe told him. "That antidote will take some time to work."

Ben and Zoe made themselves as comfortable as they could. They sat and watched the mother and cub. Rani lay down next to Prince, wrapping her long tail right around him.

"Aw," Zoe said with a sigh. "How cute."

Ben rolled his eyes. "Ugh, cuteness overload," he said. "Though I admit, Rani is a great mom. She knows how to protect her baby from the freezing air."

Rani suddenly gave a high-pitched mew and stood up, her tail swishing back and forth nervously. She nosed urgently at her cub, but Prince didn't stir.

Rani gave Prince a tap with her paw. Still there was no sign of movement.

"What's wrong?" whispered Zoe. "He's not dead, is he?"

Ben zoomed his goggles in on Prince's limp body. "I can't see if he's breathing or not," he whispered.

The twins watched anxiously for any sign of movement from the cub. Rani gulped down her kill, then she flopped to the ground and wrapped her tail around her cub again.

"Can we get any closer?" whispered Zoe. "I need to know what's wrong with him."

"No," said Ben. "We have to leave it to Rani — and the antidote."

"She doesn't seem too worried now," Zoe said. "Maybe she can tell he's healing."

Ben jerked his finger toward the leopard. "Wait, did you see that?" he asked.

"What?" Zoe asked.

Ben rapidly adjusted the zoom on his goggles. "I'm sure he twitched an ear," he said. "Look, he did it again. He's alive!"

Zoe squeezed Ben's arm. He could see that her eyes were bright with happy tears. Then she stiffened. "Prince being poisoned has really slowed us down," she said. "I wonder how the other cubs are. They need their mom, too."

Ben hit a key on his BUG. "I'll send a message to Erika and find out," he said.

The reply came quickly. "Have spotted fresh tracks, but no sighting of cubs yet," Erika's text read.

"Oh, no," said Zoe. "Do you think they died?"

"Don't despair just yet," said Ben. "Erika won't give up until she's found them." He quietly rummaged through his backpack. "I don't know about you, but I'm starving. Here, have an energy bar."

Zoe grinned as she took it from him. "You're always starving!" she said.

Before they could take a bite of their snacks, Rani suddenly jerked to her feet. She cautiously nudged her son, and the little cub raised his head. A moment later, he shakily rose to his feet.

"Look, Ben!" Zoe whispered.

Ben pulled on the nozzle of his BUG. "Yep!" he said. "Now to get them heading in the right direction."

Zoe checked her satellite map. "We're a ways off from our original route," she said. "We have to go west now."

Ben tapped a key. "I'll set it to fire the scent bomb a hundred yards west of our current position. That should get them on their way quickly."

"No more holograms," said Zoe.

Rani caught the scent right as the pellet smashed into the distant rock. She pushed Prince to go with her. He sniffed the air and gave a small mewling sound.

"I bet his instincts are kicking in," Zoe murmured. "That's great. He wants to check out the smell even though he's still weak."

Rani grabbed Prince by the scruff of his neck and set off, moving slowly and carefully over the bare rock.

Zoe called up the cub's signal on her BUG. "It's a good thing she's carrying Prince," she said. "It's slowing her down enough that we should be able to keep up with her."

They walked across the flat floor of the valley, following the leopards. Gray, jagged rocks and sheer cliff faces rose in front of them, and Rani was already climbing up toward the scent bomb.

"Time to rope ourselves together," said Zoe. "Then we can put our WILD climbing training to good use."

They slipped on their harnesses and helmets, and took out some metal spikes with holes in the end from their backpacks. Then they clipped the spikes to a ring on their belts. "We'll need these pitons handy," said Ben.

Both Zoe and Ben clipped the ends of the rope to their harnesses. Ben was soon getting into the rhythm of the climb, finding holds in the craggy rock face like it was second nature. Then he stopped, took one of his metal spikes, and rammed the point hard into a horizontal crack in the rock. "The piton's firm," he called, giving it a tug.

Ben attached a clip to it and pushed the climbing rope through its clasp. "The carabiner is firmly attached," he called out.

Zoe set off after him, cramming her gloved fingers into crevices to get good holds. She felt the strain on her muscles as she hauled herself up the rock. When she reached the first anchor point, she pulled it out and stowed it in her pocket.

The temperature was dropping as Ben and Zoe took turns climbing up. They could see their breath in a thick cloud of vapor that looked green through their night-vision glasses. The icy air made the lenses mist up and they had to keep stopping to wipe them clear.

"The goggles need little windshield wipers!" said Zoe, as she pulled herself onto another rocky shelf. Her arms and legs were aching with the effort of the climb.

"We should tell Uncle Stephen to improve the design," Ben said.

There was no more talk as they climbed higher. Instead, they focused on trying to find the safest route. They kept constant watch on the tracking signals. Whenever Rani stopped, they sent another scent bomb to lure the cats farther along their route.

Every now and then, they caught glimpses of Rani carrying her cub toward the scent.

After what seemed like hours, Ben and Zoe took a short rest on an overhang. Zoe crouched down close to her brother. They sat together, warming their bodies and numb hands.

Zoe found herself breathing heavily in the thin air. She felt dizzy, and it was coming over her in waves. She tried to convince herself that she was just tired. She decided not to tell Ben. She didn't want him to worry.

"My turn to lead," Zoe said, struggling to her feet. She made a new anchor and attached their rope to it. Then she reached out toward a crack in the rock that would give a good handhold.

It seemed to move away from her fingers. She blinked hard and went to grab it. Her hand missed and she lost her balance. The next second, she was plummeting into the darkness of the ravine. Rocks, snow, and sky whirled in front of her eyes in a terrifying blur as she fell, too shocked to scream.

"Zoe!" cried Ben.

CHAPTER 9

UNDER THE WEATHER

Ben jammed his boots against the rock face and held on to the rope with all his strength. He felt a hard jolt. For a second, he thought the force was going to pull out Zoe's anchor and send them both tumbling down the mountainside. But it seemed secure — for now. Ben carefully peered over the edge of the overhang. Zoe was dangling against the rock face, limbs flailing.

She twisted awkwardly around and looked up. "Ben!" she said feebly.

"Zoe!" Ben said, calling down to her. "You okay? I don't know how long the piton will hold, can you climb back up? I can pull you up, but you need to help me."

Zoe could just see her brother's worried face looking down at her. She tried to clear her muddled head. She reached out for the rock. As soon as her numb fingers found a handhold, Ben pulled. Zoe jammed her feet and hands into small cracks and began to climb with Ben's help.

"You took your time!" Ben said. He was grinning down at her over the edge of the rock as he held out a hand. Zoe took it, gladly, and Ben helped her up to join him on the ledge.

Zoe sat down shakily. The world was spinning before her eyes and her head was pounding. With a sinking feeling, she realized what was wrong. It wasn't the fall that had made her feel this way, or the tiredness. She'd felt like this in the climate chamber. It was altitude sickness. She knew it could be serious and that the only cure was to get down the mountain. But they couldn't do that. Rani and her cubs were too important.

"Are you all right?" asked Ben.

Zoe nodded. There were dark circles beneath her eyes.

"What happened?" Ben asked, his eyes narrowed.

"My glove must have slipped," Zoe said quietly. She stood up before he could ask more questions. "Let's get going."

Ben flicked through the BUG's menu to check the satellite map. "There's a long ridge northwest of here," he said, jabbing at the image with his glove. "It's the one that leads straight over the top of the avalanche. It's about two hours of climbing, looks like."

"Sounds good," said Zoe, trying to act normal. She checked her watch. "But dawn will be breaking in about an hour. Rani will stop then, so we'll be able to get some sleep and reach the ridge by tonight."

Ben looked up at the mountainside. "It won't be long until we're at the snowline," he said. "It's going to be even more slippery on those rocks. Remember what Erika told us on the plane? The surface of the snow melts when the sun's shining, and then it freezes again at night. We're going to be climbing on sheer ice."

Making sure their ropes were still well fastened, they set off up the steep climb. Zoe had to use all her strength to keep going. The terrain was bare rock at first, but gradually, patches of snow showed up beneath their feet. Soon there was no rock to be seen, and the whole mountainside glistened in the moonlight.

Ben hit a clip on the side of his boots and blades popped out. "We've got our own claws," he joked.

Ben jabbed the spikes into the ice to get a good grip. Then he took his ice axe out of his backpack.

Zoe did the same, continuing to follow her brother up the ice climb. Finally she hauled herself up next to him onto a wide shelf of rock and slumped to her knees, fighting away the dizziness that nearly made her tip over.

"You sure you're all right?" asked Ben.

"Y-yes," Zoe answered quickly. She pulled out her BUG. "Just checking Prince's signal."

Zoe stared blankly at the screen for a moment. "I think . . . we've almost reached them," she said weakly. "And they've stopped over there somewhere." She pointed to a hollow in the steep mountainside with a dark crevice below. "Well, they should be there according to the BUG, but I can't see them."

Ben had a look. "If the BUG says they're there, then they must be," he said. "They're probably just camouflaged."

Something stirred in the hollow. "There they are," Zoe said with relief. "They're snuggling up together. They must be settling down to sleep."

"It is their bedtime, after all," said Ben. "Look at the sky."

Above the peaks the eastern sky was beginning to lighten. Dawn was on its way.

Zoe zoomed in her goggles for a close-up view of the cub. "Rani must have found food for Prince," she said. "He looks a lot perkier — he's biting his mom's ear!"

"We'd better set an alert on the BUG
so we get a warning if they start moving
again around nightfall," Ben said. "I've
read that they sleep most of the day."

Zoe eased her backpack off her
shoulders. She longed to put her head down
and shut her eyes.

"Supper first!" said Ben. "Or is it
breakfast?" He produced two bags from a
pocket inside his snowsuit.

"Liquid sausage and beans," Ben announced. "Give the packet a squeeze, and it'll be hot in minutes."

Zoe forced the food down. It felt good to have the warm food in her belly, but she grew nauseous even looking at food.

The sky was lighter now, covered with dull gray clouds. Ben pulled out their sleeping bags and spread them under a low overhanging rock where the snow didn't reach. A little way along, their shelf disappeared in a deep ravine. He didn't want to roll over in the night and end up falling to the bottom of that. Ben rammed a piton into the rock and secured their backpacks, sleeping bags, and climbing rope to it. They crawled inside their bags, making sure that their heads were completely covered.

"What I'd give for a nice, comfy mattress," Ben said, his voice muffled by the sleeping bag. "I'd better count some sheep . . . or leopards."

But Zoe didn't answer. She was already asleep.

CHAPTER 10
ON THE EDGE

Zoe awoke with a start. The sun was low in the clear western sky, just now dipping behind the tall peaks. She could tell she had slept all day, but she didn't feel any better. There was a stabbing pain behind her eyes. For a moment, she wondered why her bed felt so hard. Then she remembered she was a long way from home.

Wearily, she prodded her brother awake.

"It's almost night," she said. "The snow leopards will be moving soon. We need to get up and make sure they go the right way."

Ben peered out from their rocky shelter and let out a gasp. "There's been another snowfall!" he said. "And it was a heavy one. We'd better be on the lookout for avalanches."

Zoe rubbed her eyes. Their ledge and the rocks around were covered in a thick layer of snow that glistened in the late afternoon sun.

Ben crawled out of his sleeping bag and stood up on the ledge to check on the snow leopards. His BUG vibrated. "Update from Erika," he said. He read the text out loud. "'Still no sign of the cubs, but some of the food is gone.'"

"Hope the cubs were the ones who ate it," muttered Zoe, holding her head in her hands.

"At least our cub has his mom with him," said Ben. He looked up the glistening white mountainside. He could see the hollow where the leopard and her cub had slept. There was one small shape curled up inside.

"Rani's not there!" Ben cried. "She left Prince on his own. Where did she go?"

When Zoe didn't answer, Ben looked over at her.

Zoe was sitting with her head in her hands. Her eyes were closed. She looked very pale.

"Are you all right?" Ben asked, looking alarmed.

Zoe couldn't hide it from him anymore. "Everything's whirling around," she said in a slow groan. "And I have an awful headache."

Ben knelt down next to her. "I bet you have altitude sickness. First things first, you need to take some acetaminophen." He dug around in his backpack and handed one to her, then gave her a drink of water. "Then we have to go down to a lower altitude until you feel better."

"I know the drill," said Zoe weakly. "But we can't go down. That would mean abandoning our mission."

"Altitude sickness can be very serious," said Ben. "If going back is what it takes to keep you safe, then that's what we have to do."

Ben swung his backpack onto his shoulders and helped Zoe put hers on. Then he pulled out the piton that had anchored them while they slept.

"No, Ben," Zoe said, almost sobbing. "We have to keep going." She looked over to the little cub. Prince was on his feet. He sniffed the air and began to climb unsteadily out of the hollow. "We can't give up now."

"We're going down and that's final," said Ben.

Ben tried to gently lift his sister by her shoulders. But Zoe was staring over his head, watching something in the air. "Look!" she said.

Ben followed her gaze to see a huge eagle circling above them, gliding silently through the air on its powerful wings.

"Yeah, that's impressive," said Ben. "But you can't change the subject like —"

"I'm not," insisted Zoe. "The eagle's out hunting . . . and it spotted Prince!"

The eagle swooped down. Talons outstretched, it was heading straight for the terrified cub. Prince let out a frightened mew and cringed back.

"We've got to do something!" yelled Zoe. She scrambled to her feet, ignoring the thumping in her head. "An eagle could easily carry away a cub."

She scrolled frantically through her BUG, trying to find something to scare the predator away.

"No time for that!" cried Ben. He grabbed a handful of snow, smashed it into a ball, and flung it at the diving eagle. It missed, but the eagle swerved away.

Prince was backing away from the attack, but behind him was a sheer drop — and he was backing dangerously close to it.

The eagle made another attack, swooping so low that it seemed sure to hit its target. Zoe cried out, expecting to see the helpless cub dangling from its talons.

But when it rose
again, its claws were
empty. It let out a harsh
cry and flew away.

"You did it!" cried Zoe.
"Prince is safe!"

But then they saw that the little cub
had disappeared.

CHAPTER 11

IN THE BAG

Ben and Zoe scrambled up to the ledge. Very carefully, they edged toward the sheer drop, afraid of seeing a dead leopard cub staring up at them. But no matter where they looked, they saw no sign of life.

Then they heard the faintest of sounds. A pitiful, high-pitched cry.

"That's Prince!" Ben said in amazement. He peered over the edge. "I can see him. He fell onto a sort of natural outcropping in the rock."

Ben reached over the edge a little farther to look closer. "But he's a long way down and I can't see any footholds," he added with a frown.

"It's up to us to rescue him," said Zoe. "And we'll have to do it before Rani returns."

"I'll climb down and pick him up," Ben suggested.

"How will you climb back?" asked Zoe. "You'll have your hands full with a cub. I mean, what if he struggles?"

"That's a good point," said Ben. "I need something to carry him in." He thought for a moment. "Got it! I'll take a sleeping bag and wrap him in that. If we tie it to my end of the rope, you can hoist him up. We'll use one of the pitons as a pulley."

Zoe nodded. "Sounds good," she said. "I'll keep an eye on you — and the other on the lookout for Rani."

Ben rolled up his sleeping bag and tucked it into his harness. Then he rammed a piton into the rock, threaded his rope through it, and steadily climbed down as Zoe let out the rope. But when he approached the ledge, the little cub backed away in fear, huddling back in the narrow end of the rock path.

Ben moved slowly down until he felt flat rock beneath his feet. Then he hesitated. If he approached Prince, the cub might panic and fall again. Ben slowly slid down to a crouching position, keeping as still as he could. Prince was watching him suspiciously, ready to leap away at any sudden movement.

Once in a while, Prince glanced anxiously at the top of the ledge, as if hoping for a glimpse of his mom.

"I'm not going to hurt you," Ben said under his breath. He unrolled the sleeping bag and opened the end wide. He slowly pulled out the nozzle on his BUG and fired a pellet into his open hand. It broke on impact, letting out a pungent smell. Ben could tell that Prince was curious by the way the cub's ears and eyes perked up. The little cub put forward one nervous paw. Then another.

It's working! Ben thought. He breathed slowly, trying to keep his excitement at bay. He had to stay calm. This was his one chance at saving Prince's life. He held his hand out flat and perfectly still, inviting the cub to come closer.

Prince was close, prowling low, but eager to reach the bait.

Then Prince placed his nose in Ben's hand. Ben moved quickly. He firmly but gently grasped a handful of soft fur on the nape of Prince's neck.

By the time Prince realized what was happening, Ben had bundled him inside the sleeping bag.

Prince struggled, mewing loudly for his mother. Ben unclipped his rope and attached it to the sleeping bag. "Ready!" he yelled to Zoe.

Ignoring the pounding in her head, Zoe pulled on the rope. Slowly, she began to lift up the heavy weight. When the wriggling sleeping bag was almost level with the ledge, she grabbed it and hauled it up next to her.

At that moment, she heard a growl behind her. Zoe whipped around, and then let out a cry of fear.

Rani was facing Zoe on the narrow ledge. The leopard must have heard her cub's calls. She was crouched, ready to pounce at any moment.

There was only one thing to do. Zoe feverishly ripped open the sleeping bag, pulled Prince out and set him on his feet. The little snow leopard spotted his mother immediately and galloped joyfully toward her with little yelps of excitement.

Forgetting all about Zoe, Rani bounded toward him. She took him by the scruff of the neck, turned, and dashed up the steep mountainside. Prince wriggled in her grasp. After a few more steps, Rani put him down and he scrambled after her.

Zoe slumped down on the ledge.

Ben's worried face appeared. "What's going on?" he demanded.

Zoe said nothing. Ben climbed up onto the ledge. "I heard you yell!" he said. "Where's Prince?"

"His mom came to pick him up," said Zoe, managing a wobbly grin. "But I don't know if they're going the right way."

"We'll just have to hope they are," said Ben, clipping himself back on to the rope. "We've got to get you down the mountain now. No arguing."

With fumbling hands, Zoe took out her BUG. "Look," she said, shakily holding up the satellite image to her brother. "We're so close to the avalanche site. We only have to get over the top, and we'll be back in Rani's home territory. Erika can pick us up there after we've gotten them home safe."

Ben hesitated. "It may be close," he said, "but the next part wouldn't be easy even if you were perfectly healthy. We have to get to that narrow path above the snowfield left behind by the avalanche. It'll involve lots of tough climbing — and everything's covered in snow now, so it's going to be slippery. What if you fall again?"

"I won't," said Zoe firmly. She lifted her BUG, and flicked to the snow leopards' signals. "We can't risk letting them go back alone now. I'm going to fire another scent bomb to make sure they're on track."

Ben sighed. He knew it was no good to argue with his sister once her mind was set on something. But he didn't like that his sister was putting the snow leopards' safety before her own.

It was very dark, so they both pulled on their night-vision goggles. Ben began to climb, his sister roped firmly to him. The deep, fresh snow made it difficult to find firm holds on the rock, even with their ice axes.

They stopped frequently to aim scent bombs farther up the mountainside. Now that Prince was recovered from the poison, it was becoming harder to keep the two snow leopards from heading off in the wrong direction. The agile cats could move much faster than Ben and Zoe through the treacherous Himalayan terrain. And now, it was snowing again.

Ben could sense that Zoe's strength was giving out. Only sheer determination was keeping her going.

And then he spotted a wonderful sight.

"We've reached the avalanche field!" Ben called over his shoulder.

"Are you sure?" said Zoe. She hauled herself up behind him and gasped.

Ahead, stretching as far as they could see, a smooth carpet of snow covered the steep slope . . . and it was untouched by any animal prints.

Ben used the zoom on his goggles and scanned the peaks above. "There's our path, running along the top of it," he said. "Right across the steepest slope."

Zoe looked up at the heavy snow-covered peaks looming above them. She wiped the snowflakes from her goggles and just managed to suppress a groan of exhaustion at the thought of the climb ahead.

"We've just got to get Rani along that ridge," said Ben, "and hopefully she'll sense her home — and her other cubs. I'm sure Erika will have found them by now."

Ben checked Rani and her cub's signals. They were moving slowly across the rocks directly north from where Ben and Zoe were standing.

Ben took his ice axe out of his backpack. "It's not going to take much to get them on the right path now," he said. "I'll go. You wait here, I'll come back for you."

Zoe shook her head. "We have to stay together," she said, her lips tight.

Ben sighed. He checked the rope that tied them together and grinned at her. "I'm making sure this is secure, just in case you decide to take another spontaneous nap."

Reaching up with his left hand, Ben slammed an axe into the ice-covered rock. He used it to steady himself while he found footholds. He pulled himself up a bit, then did the same again. He could feel the rope tugging on his harness as Zoe struggled to keep going. He slowed the pace and held the rope taut to take some of her weight. Every now and then, he caught a glimpse of Rani and Prince up ahead, following the trail of the scent bombs.

He stopped to check his BUG. As Zoe climbed up beside him, he showed her the screen. "Look," he said.

Zoe strained her eyes to focus on the leopards' signals on the satellite map. "They've reached the ridge!" she exclaimed. "They're almost home."

"And we're almost there too," said Ben.

"I'll race you then," said Zoe with a feeble chuckle. "As long as you give me a push first!"

Once on the ridge, Ben put their ice axes away. "We don't need these now," he said. "This part will be like an easy hike."

Zoe let out a sigh of relief. She stumbled along behind him. Now that they weren't climbing, she was finding it easier to breathe, although her headache wasn't getting any better.

Their mission was nearly over. Suddenly, they heard Rani let out a yowl somewhere ahead.

Zoe gripped Ben's arm. "Do you think she picked up the scent of her other cubs?" she said with excitement.

"She sounded scared," Ben said.

Another sound reached their ears. "What's that?" whispered Zoe, puzzled. "It's like a deep drumbeat."

White swirls billowed up from the peaks above. An immense hissing sound filled the air as waves of snow came pounding down toward them.

"It's an avalanche!" cried Zoe. "And Rani and Prince are right in its path!"

"So are we!" yelled Ben.

CHAPTER 12

AVALANCHE!

Ben and Zoe were engulfed in a wave of powdery snow. "Get to the side!" Ben yelled. The force swept them off their feet, threatening to turn them over and over.

Ben struggled, kicked, and thrashed against the power of the avalanche, trying to get to the edge of the flow. His mouth filled with icy flakes as be breathed heavily.

After a while, the flow slowed. His feet touched firmer snow beneath him and he was able to wade through the drifts.

At this point, Ben was very glad he'd paid attention during the avalanche training on the plane.

The rope on his harness was getting tight. That meant that Zoe hadn't kept up with his pace, and was likely being overwhelmed by the force of the snow. He had to help her. He reached out for a large boulder and pulled himself up. He was out of the avalanche.

Gasping for breath, he made sure he had a good foothold and pulled on the rope. He could just see Zoe's flailing arms. He pulled harder and saw her struggle toward him. She was waist deep now and seemed to have found her footing, but she looked very tired.

"We're almost there, Zoe," Ben called.

Suddenly, there was another deep rumble from high on the mountain. Ben looked up the slope and saw a huge wave of snow moving much faster than the first. It pounded down, sending up a frosty spray behind it. Zoe was right in its path.

Ben knew the force of the snow would pull her under and that would drag him in, too. Still, Ben refused to let go.

Then he felt the rope go loose. Zoe had unclipped herself.

"No! Zoe!" Ben cried out.

* * *

WHAM! The avalanche was upon Zoe. At once, she was smothered by icy snow. She went tumbling over and over, the sound of the snow pounding in her ears.

Zoe felt completely helpless in the immense power of the avalanche. Then she heard Ben cry out for her. Suddenly, a new determination seized her.

She kicked out again, using every bit of her remaining strength to swim through the snow once more. But it was no good. Even if she hadn't gotten altitude sickness, she knew she couldn't hope to overcome the incredible force of the snow.

Remembering the training film, she forced her aching arms up and cupped her hands in front of her face. Now at least she'd have a little air supply if she was buried.

After what seemed like forever, she realized that she'd stopped moving. The avalanche must have run its course.

It was pitch black now. The snow was pressing down on her. It would soon start to harden, and then it would suffocate her.

"Get digging!" Zoe told herself.

First, she had to figure out which way was up. She'd lost all sense of direction. Zoe scratched at the snow in front of her face and felt it fall onto her nose. That meant she was lying face up.

She stretched her hand toward the surface, but all she felt was more snow. The realization hit her like a punch: she was buried deep. There was no point using up her air and energy trying to dig. The training video had said she would have about fifteen minutes of air. She hoped that would be enough.

She had to set off the FANG on her helmet to alert Ben. Then her blood ran cold. She had no idea if he'd escaped.

The snow was already hardening around her. She had to get her head in the right position to aim the FANG toward the surface, and she had to do it now before the weight of the avalanche crushed her.

It was her only hope. She couldn't reach her BUG since it was tucked deep in her pocket.

Zoe forced herself to take slow breaths, but she could hardly move her arms. How was she going to pull the cord on her harness? She tried to jab down with one elbow. The snow resisted, making her feel the pain in her muscles as she forced her arm back down.

At last, one finger touched the ring on the end of the cord, but she couldn't get a grip on it. She tried again, jerking her arm down through the wall of snow. At last her finger caught the ring. Her helmet shuddered as the FANG fired. She could hear a muffled whoosh as it sped away. Then she felt a cold pinprick of air on her neck. She had an air supply! The FANG had reached the surface and its beacon would be giving out a warning light.

But is Ben there to see it? she wondered.

* * *

Ben felt sick with dread as he reeled in the loose rope. As quickly as it had begun, the avalanche stopped. Silence fell again. He desperately scanned the deep snow field. There was no sign of his sister anywhere.

WOOSH! His head whipped around at a rocket-like sound. He saw the end of Zoe's FANG shooting into the air a little ways down the slope. It flew up to the end of its wire and the fluorescent orange umbrella opened and fell to the ground. The beacon on its point began to flash.

"There she is!" Ben cried out.

Now he knew where to dig, but he had to get there safely first. He lay flat on the new snow. "I have to spread my weight out," he muttered to himself.

Ben sank a little. That meant the snow was already freezing and compacting. He scrabbled toward the FANG umbrella. He held it tightly and gave it two sharp tugs to let Zoe know he was at the other end.

He knew his sister didn't have long. Ben began to dig, hacking at the hardened snow with his ice axes, following the line of the FANG. But it was taking too long. The hole didn't seem to be getting any deeper, and snow kept tumbling back down into it. Suddenly, he saw a slight movement below him as Zoe's gloved hand forced its way out. Ben grabbed her fingers and gave them a squeeze.

He dug frantically, throwing the snow out behind him. At last, Zoe's head emerged. Then her shoulders. With one final tug, Ben dragged her out through the snow.

At last, Zoe was free from her snowy prison. Ben hugged her, unable to speak from exhaustion and relief. Then he began to rub her arms and legs to warm her up.

"Thanks," said Zoe simply, her teeth chattering with cold.

As soon as she could move, they crawled to the edge of the snowfield.

"We've made it to the snow leopards' territory," said Ben with a grin. "Though not quite the way we hoped to."

Zoe grabbed his arm. "But what about Rani and Prince?" she asked.

SAFE AND SOUND

Ben and Zoe looked at each other. Neither of them spoke. Had the two snow leopards been swept away in the avalanche? Were they suffocating under hundreds of square feet of deadly snow?

Fingers trembling, Ben scrolled through the menu on his BUG searching for the leopards' signals. At last two flashing lights on the screen popped up. Ben and Zoe high-fived each other excitedly.

"They're moving," said Zoe. "That means that they're not buried."

"And they're not far away, either," said Ben. He looked up the slope to a small clump of birch trees. "Just beyond there."

They scrambled up the steep slope. Zoe's head was still spinning. She stumbled. Ben grabbed her arm and steadied her.

The moon had risen now and the sky was clear of clouds. Moonlight shined down upon the snow, making it sparkle. Ben bent down and inspected the ground.

"Tracks," he said. "Leading away from the avalanche to the clump of trees. Look! An adult and a cub. That's them."

They crept forward. The trees gave way to a small clearing. Zoe saw a movement ahead, and pulled Ben down out of sight.

In the middle of the clearing stood Rani with Prince by her side. She was sniffing at something on the snow-covered ground.

Suddenly, she lifted her head and gave a low mewing sound. And then she was off across the mountain, Prince bounding along behind her.

"She's tracking something," said Ben. "What is it?" He ran over to some marks in the snow. "They're snow leopard tracks," he called. "There are two sets, and they're definitely not adult. I think they're even smaller than Prince's prints are!"

Zoe came up to him, a huge grin on her face. "It has to be the missing cubs!" she said. "Let's go, I can't miss this."

They didn't have to go far. Hiding under a rock outcropping, Rani was pushing and nuzzling at three wriggling cubs.

"They're all safe!" said Zoe, her eyes shining as she watched the babies climbing all over their mother.

Ben looked at his sister and laughed softly. He could see by her expression that Zoe was under the influence of cuteness overload. *She deserves to be happy after all she did,* he thought.

Rani gave each of her cubs a good lick. "Aw, Prince is playing with his mother's tail," whispered Zoe. "He's definitely bigger than the others."

"It looks like the other two are girls," said Ben. The two little ones jumped on each other in a mock fight.

Then Rani stood up. "I think she's content now that they're all safe," said Zoe. "It must be wonderful for her to be home again."

"Time for us to go home, too," said Ben.

They waited until Rani had moved farther up the slope, her cubs jostling each other as they followed. Then Zoe hit the BUG's hot key to call Erika.

"Am I glad to hear from you!" came her voice. "I just flew over and saw the fresh avalanche. Are you both all right?"

"Better than all right," said Zoe. "Mission accomplished! Rani and Prince are back where they belong."

"And Rani found her other two cubs," said Ben. "They're looking good. Your food drops must have kept them going."

"Wonderful!" Erika exclaimed. "I'll send you coordinates for a pick-up point. I'm afraid it will be farther down the mountain, though."

Zoe suddenly realized how sick she felt now that the excitement was over. "Down's good," she told Erika, a weak smile on her face.

WILD VICTORY

Inside the warm plane, Ben and Zoe dug in to plates of steaming rice and chicken. Now that she was in a pressurized cabin, Zoe was beginning to feel better.

"I'll just do a final flyby to check on Rani and the cubs," Erika said from the cockpit. "Since it's not light yet, we'll have to use the heat-seeking monitor. Check it for me, please."

Erika turned the plane in a slow dive.

They passed over the protected area. Ben and Zoe watched the monitor closely. Soon, small red shapes appeared. "Rodents," said Ben.

Then something flashed across the screen. "That was a goat, I think," added Zoe. "There's plenty of food for our snow leopards tonight."

And then they saw them. One large red glow next to three smaller ones, huddling in the safety of a rocky den.

Zoe checked the BUG for Prince's signal. "That's them," she said happily.

Ben nodded. "Aw," he said. "I bet they're all curled up with Rani's tail wrapped around them."

Zoe laughed. "Now who's the one experiencing cuteness overload?"

Ben blushed. "Whatever," he said.

Erika took the plane out of its dive and they flew away over the majestic peaks of the Himalayas.

Ben pulled out his BUG and clicked the key for WILD HQ.

"I've been waiting on pins and needles for your call," boomed Uncle Stephen's voice. "How'd it go?"

"Mission accomplished!" said Ben. "All the leopards are home where they belong."

"Excellent!" said their uncle. "Hurry back. I want you to try out the sunny beach setting in the climate chamber!"

"Cool!" cried Zoe. "We're on our way!"

Zoe caught Ben's eye. They grinned at each other. Being a WILD operative was just about the best thing in the world.

THE AUTHORS

Jan Burchett and **Sara Vogler** were already friends when they discovered they both wanted to write children's books, and that it was much more fun to do it together. They have since written over a hundred and thirty stories ranging from educational books and stories for younger readers to young adult fiction. They have written for series such as Dinosaur Cove and Beast Quest, and they are authors of the Gargoylz books.

THE ILLUSTRATOR

Diane Le Feyer discovered a passion for drawing and animation at the age of five. In 2002, she graduated with honors from the Ecole Emile Cohl school of design. Diane worked as a character designer, 3D modeler, and animator in the video games industry before joining the Cartoon Saloon animation studio, where she worked as a director, animator, illustrator, and character designer. Diane was also a part of the early design and development of the movie *The Secret of Kells*.

GLOSSARY

altitude (AL-ti-tood)—the height of something above sea level

avalanche (AV-uh-lanch)—a large mass of snow, ice, or earth that suddenly moves down the side of a mountain

endangered (en-DAYN-jurd)—in danger or threatened

extinct (ek-STINGKT)—if a plant or animal has gone extinct, then it has died out

habitation (hab-i-TAY-shuhn)—a home or dwelling

massive (MASS-iv)—large, heavy, or solid

mountaineer (moun-tuh-NEER)—someone who climbs mountains

piton (PEE-tahn)—a metal spike that looks like a big needle that is used to connect rope to while climbing.

terrain (tuh-RAYN)—ground or land

threatened (THRET-uhnd)—at risk of harm

treacherous (TRECH-ur-uhss)—not to be trusted, or dangerous

The snow leopard lives in the mountainous regions of Central Asia at altitudes of up to 20,000 feet. They will descend to 6,000 feet to hunt prey. They are around 6 feet long, and half of that length is their long tails.

HUNTING: Snow leopards are sometimes hunted for their bones, which are used in some traditional Chinese medicines. They are also trapped for their fur, despite the practice being banned. Herders sometimes hunt the leopards that kill their domesticated livestock, since those herders depend on their livestock for survival.

HOSTILE HABITAT: Snow leopards live in an extremely dangerous environment. While they are incredibly agile and sure-footed, the harsh weather and slippery surfaces mean a single misstep can cause them to fall to their deaths.

BUT IT'S NOT ALL BAD FOR THE SNOW LEOPARD! Snow leopards have had protected status in India for over 50 years now. The use of snow leopard fur is illegal. Many conservation organizations work with local inhabitants to help protect the snow leopard from being hunted, by teaching herders how to better protect their livestock. In some areas, people are given money as compensation when a snow leopard kills their livestock.

DISCUSSION QUESTIONS

1. Ben and Zoe often have to lie to people about their missions in order to make sure they succeed. Is it ever okay to lie? Why or why not?

2. The twins love animals. What's your favorite animal? Why?

3. Zoe and Ben have to work together to be successful in their missions. Talk about times when you've had to team up with others.

WRITING PROMPTS

1. Zoe gets caught under a lot of snow after an avalanche. Write a short story told from her perspective about what she feels and thinks as she struggles to find her way out.

2. Uncle Stephen trusts his nephew and niece, Ben and Zoe, to perform important tasks for him. Has an adult ever asked you to do something important? Write about a time when someone asked you for help.

3. Write your own WILD Rescue adventure! Where do you go? What animal do you save? What kinds of cool gadgets do you use during your mission? Write about it.

READ ALL OF BEN & ZOE'S
WILD ADVENTURES!

VISIT:
CAPSTONEPUB.COM

1. WILD RESCUE — POACHER PANIC
2. WILD RESCUE — EARTHQUAKE ESCAPE
3. WILD RESCUE — RAINFOREST RESCUE
4. WILD RESCUE — POLAR MELTDOWN
5. WILD RESCUE — SAFARI SURVIVAL
6. WILD RESCUE — OCEAN S.O.S.
7. WILD RESCUE — AVALANCHE ALERT
8. WILD RESCUE — DESERT DANGER

FIND COOL WEBSITES
AND MORE BOOKS LIKE THIS ONE AT
FACTHOUND.COM

JUST TYPE IN THE BOOK ID:
9781434237729
AND YOU'RE READY TO GO!